BUNNIE THE BUNNY
2IN1
BUNNIE AND BUGSY

Gary Paul Stephenson

Pharos Books

ISBN: 978-93-95862-89-9

Publisher: Pharos Books (P) Ltd.
Plot No.-55, Main Mother Dairy Road
Pandav Nagar, East Delhi-110092 (India)
Phone: +014049995474
WhatsApp: +014049995474
E-mail: sales@pharosbooks.in
Website: www.pharosbooks.in
Edition: 2023

Printed By: Sushma Book Binding House, Okhla
Industrial Area, Phase II, New Delhi-110020

BUNNIE THE BUNNY 2-in-1 BUNNIE AND BUGSY
Author: Gary Paul Stephenson

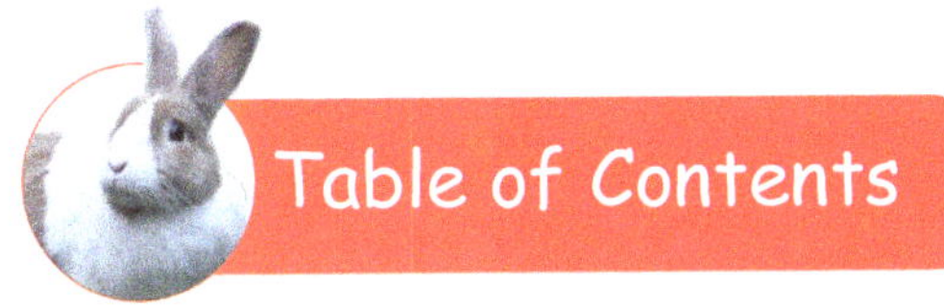

Table of Contents

BUNNIE THE BUNNY

Chapter One

When I first arrived home I was so scared. I was alone in a dark box and when the top was opened it was so bright and these giant hands came towards me and picked me up.

They were gentle hands that placed me in a large hutch with a soft floor and fresh water and hay. I even had a small white teddy bear. I watched as they opened another box and lifted my brother out - he panicked - I tried to tell him it was okay but he would not listen. I heard him placed in the room above mine. I told him it was okay. These were nice people.

At least we were together in the same house.

Chapter Two

After a short while we were taken to the doctor, who they called vets, who examined us and gave us each an injection which, ouch, hurt a little bit. Then one day my brother disappeared for the day, I was so lonely. When he came home he did not say anything, he just slept for a while. The following day I was whisked away and found myself back at the vets. I do not remember the day, only waking up at home feeling sleepy and seeing the fur from my tummy was gone.

Chapter Three

Meeting my Brother

After our visits to the doctor, who they called vets, our owners let us relax and eat fresh vegetables and herbs from their garden and play in our play area, but not together which I could not understand.

My brother was naughty and kept trying to get into my room. Then one day our humans let us both into the play area together, I was so happy, I met my brother for the first time in 3 months.

We sat beside each other and talked about the vet visit and the food and hay we were given and decided it was going to be a good family to stay with.

Chapter Four

The Big Outdoors

Our human owners, who we now called our servants, moved to a new home and made us a lovely outdoor pen to play in. It was wonderful to feel the grass under our feet for the very first time and the wind in our ears and have the room to run and hop, stretch in the sun and eat fresh grass. When water fell from the sky they picked us up and took us back in the dry home where we were allowed to roam every room.

Chapter Five

Freedom

My brother is so lazy, when outside in the sun, rather than running around and playing games with me, he just lies down and bathes in the sunshine. He loves the outdoors till a bird or airplane flies overhead, he then runs inside so fast I could laugh. I slowly follow him with a bit more dignity.

Chapter Six

When it rains our humans, ,our servants, keep us inside with boxes and toys to play with. During the day when inside we sleep and relax in our bedroom. Until it is time to eat. At lunchtime we always get some banana which is our favourite snack.

Chapter Seven

Eating

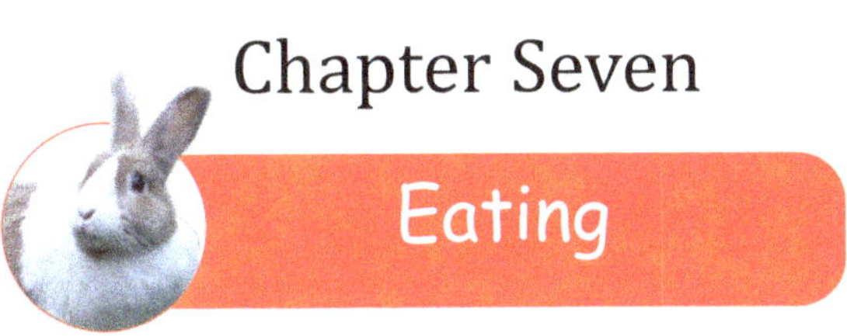

Eating is one of our favourite pastimes and we often steal from each other's plates. We love our food of fresh greens and especially like banana's.

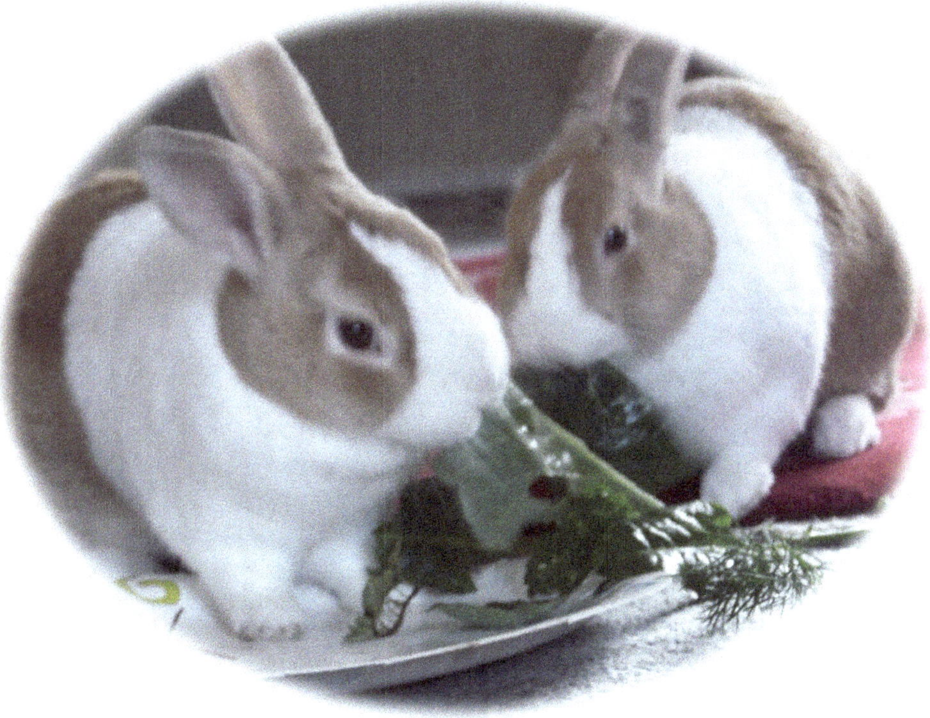

After breakfast, lunch and dinner, we flop on our side and sleep.

Any place we can.....

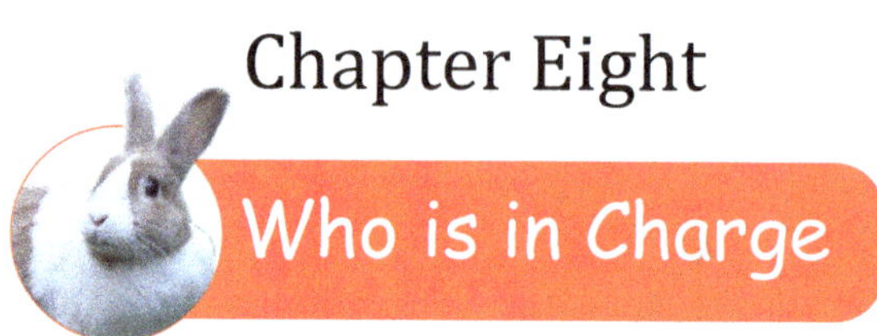
Chapter Eight

Who is in Charge

Our human owners, our servants, like to think they are in charge. But what they do not know is that we are in charge. Especially when we want something. They cannot resist us.

Sometimes we have to have a good talk about how best to get our servants to do what we want!

But mostly, I'm the boss, I'm the Bunnie..

Chapter Nine

Togetherness

But whatever happens, the most important things is, we have each other.

BUNNIE AND BUGSY

Hi, I am Bunnie the bunny. I am an apricot and white Dutch house rabbit. This means I live in a house just like you do. I live with two humans who I know as my mum and dad. I roam freely round the house during the day where I have various places where I like to go to play or rest.

If the weather is warm and dry, then I can go into the back garden where I like to eat grass. Grass is one of my favorite foods. Do you have a favorite food? Besides eating grass, I like to dig in the dirt or if the sandbox is set up, I dig and then flop in the sand. Flopping is where I just throw myself down onto my side. I do not hurt myself.

I have a brother called Bugsy. We keep each other company. We like to groom each other's ears, back and neck. Bugsy and I are great friends. We enjoy our time together. At night when we go to sleep, we go into our own bedroom where we stay all night. Here we have fresh Timothy hay to eat and fresh water to drink. Timothy hay is dried grass and is the best hay a rabbit can eat. Everyday our dad brushes our fur which gets rid of any loose strands. Just like you brush or comb your hair. In the house we have play areas made from cardboard boxes and tunnels to run along. Inside the boxes we have fresh hay to eat or to cuddle down into to have a nap.

Bugsy and I know what time of day it is. Can you tell the time? At 7.30am in the morning it is breakfast time and I sit by the bedroom door waiting for my mum to let me out. Bugsy and I each have our own food bowls and we have a small amount of rabbit pellets in these bowls for us to eat followed by special medicines to keep us well. These pellets are nice and crunchy. At lunchtime, it is banana time. Banana is my number one all-time favorite food. When I smell the banana, I get so excited that I cannot sit still and run around my dad's chair. We just have a small slice each. At teatime I sit by the TV and Bugsy sits by the armchair waiting for our food bowls with a small amount of rabbit pellets in ready for us to eat. Afterwards we again have special medicines to keep us well. At bedtime Bugsy and I assume our positions in front of the TV and armchair waiting for our room to be set up for us to go to sleep. Bugsy and I drink a special multi vitamin drink and we eat a special Timothy hay block which helps to settle us down. A Timothy hay block contains compressed Timothy hay with added herbs and flowers for extra flavor. Do you have supper? A drink and a biscuit? Bugsy and I have a cuddle before our mum and dad turn out the light ready for us to go to sleep.

In the summer we have cool mats to lie on so that we do not get too hot. In winter we have warm fluffy mats that keeps us snug. We also have the benefit of a heat pad to cuddle around. I enjoy warming my toes on it! I sit with my front paws on the heat pad and my rear paws just resting on the edge.

Every day our dad cleans and tidies up our bedroom to keep us healthy. This means cleaning out our litter trays and refreshing our hay and water. A litter tray is where Bugsy and I go to the bathroom when we are in the house. You would go to the bathroom

Every year we visit our vet to have an injection of a special vaccine for rabbits called Filavie that stops a virus from making us terribly ill. Our vet is so gentle that Bugsy and I do not feel a thing. A vet is an animal doctor. Are you scared of injections? When Bugsy and I need to visit the vet, our dad fastens a pet carrier onto the back seat of the car by a seat belt. Our dad sprays a special spray onto the blanket in the bottom of our carrier that helps Bugsy and I to remain quiet and not get upset.

Sunday is 'weigh' day when Bugsy and I have our weight checked to make sure that we are not losing or gaining too much weight. I must be careful with my diet whereas Bugsy is able to eat all he wants. Our ideal weight is below 2.2kg. I tend to hover around 2.1kg whereas Bugsy is around 1.9kg. Do you know your weight?

When Bugsy and I want to say hello to you,
then we use our nose to touch or bump your
body. We do not make sounds like a dog that
barks or growls, or like a cat that meows. The
only sound we occasionally make is like a grunt
and that usually means that we are not happy
or there is something worrying us. Bugsy

and I are known as prey animals, so we do not like people to hold us for any length of time. A prey animal is where another animal hunts us for food. When we are on the ground however, Bugsy and I enjoy having a stroke or just enjoying being with each other

Bugsy and I are quiet animals and we do not like too much noise. When the planes from the local airport or the police helicopter come over our garden we sometimes run into the house or to our rabbit villa at the end of the garden until they have gone. Our villa is like a dog kennel.

Bugsy and I have toys to play with, but we are quite happy just eating grass or sitting on the deck resting.

Bugsy and I have toys to play with, but we are quite happy just eating grass or sitting on the deck resting.

Although Bugsy and I enjoy each other's company we sometimes go into different rooms to rest. I like to sit or lay under the dining room table whereas Bugsy likes to go into the cardboard boxes in our bedroom for peace and quiet.

SEE OUR WEBSITE ON YOUR PERSONAL DEVICE PLEASE SCAN BELOW

Available here:

amazon Flipkart +14049995474

+91 8368220032, 011 40395855

Email: sales@pharosbooks.in

Website: www.pharosbooks.in